Karen's Lemonade Stand

Look for these
and other books about Karen
in the
Baby-sitters Little Sister series:

Little Sister

Karen's Lemonade Stand
Ann M. Martin

Illustrations by Susan Tang

A
LITTLE APPLE
PAPERBACK

SCHOLASTIC INC.
New York Toronto London Auckland Sydney

The author gratefully acknowledges
Stephanie Calmenson
for her help
with this book.

ISBN 0-590-25997-0

Copyright © 1995 by Ann M. Martin. All rights reserved. Published by Scholastic Inc. APPLE PAPERBACKS and THE BABY-SITTERS LITTLE SISTER are registered trademarks of Scholastic Inc.

12 11 10 9 8 7 6 5 4 3 2 1   5 6 7 8 9/9 0/0

Printed in the U.S.A.   40

First Scholastic printing, August 1995

Weather Report

"We are in the middle of a major heat wave, Connecticut. The temperature is ninety-two degrees and climbing. The humidity is high at eighty-three percent."

It was a Monday afternoon in early August. I was in the TV room at the big house. (I have two houses — a big house and a little house. I will tell you about them later.) My little brother, Andrew, came in and sat down next to me. (Andrew is four going on five.)

"Why are you watching the weather

channel?" he asked. "We already know it is hot outside."

"I am watching Margie Simon, the weather reporter," I replied. "I may want to be a weather reporter some day."

Hi. I am Karen Brewer. I am seven years old. I have blonde hair, blue eyes, and some freckles. Oh, yes. I wear glasses. I even have two pairs. I wear my blue pair for reading. I wear my pink pair the rest of the time.

Nannie poked her head into the TV room. (Nannie is my stepgrandmother. She helps take care of everyone at the big house. I love her a lot.)

"I am going to the supermarket to pick up a few things for dinner. Would either of you like to come along?" she asked.

"No, thank you," said Andrew.

"Is Kristy going to stay and watch us?" I asked.

Kristy is my big stepsister. She is thirteen and the best stepsister in the whole world. She is also an excellent baby-sitter. She is

2

even president of a baby-sitting club she runs with her friends. If Kristy was staying home, so was I.

"Yes, Kristy is staying here. She is in the living room with Emily Michelle," replied Nannie.

Emily Michelle is my adopted sister. She is two and a half. She is very sweet.

"I am going to stay home, too," I said.

Maybe I would practice my weather reporting. I found my sisters in the living room. Kristy was reading Emily a book. The book was called *Animal Sleepyheads*. It is a counting book.

"Ili, Karen," said Kristy. "Would you like a turn reading to Emily?"

"Sure," I replied.

I read the pages about elephants, kangaroos, and tigers. Just as we finished the book, David Michael walked in. He is my stepbrother. He is seven.

"Hi," I said. "You are just in time for my weather report."

"I know what the weather is," said David

Michael. "It is hot. It is too hot to be out-side."

"You need the full weather picture," I said. "Later in the week cool breezes may swoop in from the north."

Then again, they might not, I thought.

"I wish it would cool off by tomorrow," said Kristy. "I want to have softball practice in the afternoon."

Kristy is the coach of a softball team. It is called Kristy's Krushers. I am on the team. So are Andrew, David Michael, and some of my friends.

"Hello, everybody! We are home," called Daddy.

Daddy was home from a business meet-ing. (He works at home, though.) And Eliz-abeth had come home from her job. (She is my stepmother.) Sam and Charlie walked in behind them. (They are my big step-brothers. They are so old they are in high school.)

Goody. Now I had a big audience for my weather update.

4

2

Two Houses

Remember I told you I have two houses? Now I will tell you why.

When I was really little, I lived at the big house here in Stoneybrook, Connecticut, with Mommy, Daddy, and Andrew. Then Mommy and Daddy started fighting a lot. They told Andrew and me they loved us very much. But they could not get along with each other anymore. So Mommy and Daddy got divorced.

Mommy moved with my brother and me into a little house not too far away. Then she met Seth. Mommy and Seth got married. So Seth is our stepfather. That means the people in our little-house family are Mommy, Seth, Andrew, and me. We have pets, too. They are Midgie, Seth's dog; Rocky, Seth's cat; Emily Junior, my pet rat (she is named after Emily Michelle); and Bob, Andrew's hermit crab.

Daddy stayed at the big house after the divorce. (It is the house he grew up in.) Then he met Elizabeth and they got married. So Elizabeth is my stepmother. Elizabeth was married once before, and she had four kids — David Michael, Kristy, Sam, and Charlie.

I already told you that Emily was adopted. But I did not tell you where she was adopted from. She came from a faraway country called Vietnam.

After Emily was adopted, Nannie came to live at the big house to help out.

That means there are ten people at the big house whenever Andrew and I are there. (We switch houses every month.)

There are pets, too. They are Shannon, David Michael's big Bernese mountain dog puppy; Boo-Boo, Daddy's cranky old cat; Crystal Light the Second, my goldfish; and Goldfishie, Andrew's elephant. (Ha! I bet you know what Goldfishie really is.) Wait. I forgot to tell you that Emily Junior and Bob live at the big house whenever Andrew and I are there.

I have a special name for Andrew and me. I call us Andrew Two-Two and Karen Two-Two. (I got that name from a book my teacher read to my class. It is called *Jacob Two-Two Meets the Hooded Fang*.) I call us those names because we have two houses and two families, two mommies and two daddies, two cats and two dogs. We have two of many other things, one at each house. (That makes moving back and forth between our houses a lot easier.) We have two sets of toys and clothes and books. I have two bicycles. Andrew has two tricycles. I have two stuffed cats. Goosie lives at the little house. Moosie lives at the big house. I even have two best friends. Nancy Dawes lives next door to the little house. Hannie Papadakis lives across the street and one house down from the big house. (Nancy and Hannie and I are in the same class at school. We call ourselves the Three Musketeers.)

Now you know why I have two houses. Sometimes I miss the people in one house when I am at the other. But most of the time I am too busy having fun. So if you are wondering if I like having two houses, the answer is Y-E-S!

Karen's Lemonade Stand

"Do you want to come out and play?" asked Hannie.

It was Tuesday morning. Hannie was standing at the front door with a jump rope in her hand.

"Sure," I replied. "I will get my jump rope, too."

We started jumping in the backyard. First we sang, "Cinderella, dressed in yellow." Then we sang "Ballerina in a show, ballerina point your toe."

Next we acted out, "Teddy Bear, Teddy

Bear, turn around. Teddy Bear, Teddy Bear, touch the ground!"

I touched the ground. Then I sprawled out on the steamy grass. So did Hannie.

"It is too hot to jump rope," I said. "We need to go inside."

What a relief! The big house has central air conditioning. It felt great.

"Let's have a Lovely Ladies tea party," said Hannie.

This sounded like a good idea to me. We set up the tea party in the playroom. We invited several of my dolls. We asked the dolls how they were. They were fine. We took a few sips of make-believe tea. It was make-believe tasty. But we were not having a very good time.

"It is summer," I said. "We should be outside."

"You are right," said Hannie. "Dolls, would you like to go outside with us?"

They said yes. We took them to a shady spot in the yard. But it was hot even in the shade. Too hot.

10

"I am afraid my dolls are going to melt," I said.

"Inside is better," agreed Hannie.

We moved inside. Then outside. Then inside. And outside. Inside we were bored. Outside we were hot. Finally it was time for Hannie to go home. After she left, Charlie walked in.

"I am *so thirsty*," he said. "It is ninety-nine degrees outside."

"It feels like a million degrees," I said.

That gave me an idea. Whoever was outside was going to be thirsty because it was so hot. What do thirsty people like to drink? Lemonade! Where were they going to get this lemonade? From me! I decided to open up my very own lemonade stand. This would be gigundoly fun.

I told Nannie my idea. She liked it a lot.

"Do we have any lemonade mix?" I asked.

"It is in the cupboard near the refrigerator," Nannie replied. "Let me know if you need any help."

I found the can of lemonade and a pitcher in the cupboard. The directions on the can were for making one glass, one quart, or one gallon of lemonade. I was not sure how much a quart or a gallon was. So I made the lemonade one glass at a time and poured it into the pitcher. I made sure to leave room for lots of ice.

Next I went upstairs and made a beautiful sign with great big letters in different colors. I drew a border of lemons around the letters. The sign said, *Karen's Lemonade, 10¢ a cup*. (I did not care much about making money. I just wanted to have fun.)

There were only a few things left to do. I dragged a card table outside.

"Are you okay down there?" called Nannie.

(I had bumped into a few walls on the way out. I guess Nannie thought the house was falling down.)

"I am okay," I replied.

I carried out a chair. I brought out napkins and cups. (I put a rock on top of the

12

napkins so they would not fly away if a breeze came along.) I taped my beautiful sign to the table. Finally I carried out my ice cold pitcher of lemonade.

I sat down to wait for my first customer. This was my grand opening.

4

Waiting

I had been outside for about half an hour when Nannie brought me a peanut butter sandwich.

"I did not think you wanted to leave your business for lunch. So I brought lunch to you," said Nannie.

Then she handed me ten cents for a cup of lemonade. This was my very first sale.

"How does it taste?" I asked.

"This lemonade is delicious!" Nannie replied. "And I love the sign you made."

"Thank you," I said.

After Nannie went inside two cars passed by. But they did not stop. I guess they did not see me.

I was sure my second customer would come along soon. My second customer would tell a third customer about my delicious lemonade. The third customer would tell a fourth customer. The fourth customer would tell a fifth customer. I could see the line forming now.

But I did not get a second customer very soon. The neighborhood was practically a ghost town. I had been outside for an hour and only two people had passed by. I knew it was because it was so hot. People were in their houses with their fans or air conditioners.

I waited and waited. Then Nannie came outside again.

"That lemonade was the best I ever tasted," she said. "I would like to buy another cup."

Nannie handed me a dime. That made her my first and my second customer.

16

A few minutes later, Hannie and her brother, Linny, ran across the street. (Linny is nine going on ten.)

"How is business?" asked Linny.

"It is a little quiet. But I am sure it will pick up soon," I replied.

"I would like to buy two cups," said Hannie.

Hannie and Linny drank their lemonade. Then they had to leave. Their parents were taking them and their little sister, Sari, to the library. (Sari is Emily's age.) A trip to the library sounded like fun. It would be nice and cool there. Hannie could read a book about igloos.

I sat by myself thinking about cool things. I waited and waited. No one came for a long, long time.

Beep, beep! I jumped to my feet. Charlie and Sam were pulling into the driveway in Charlie's Junk Bucket. (That is what we call his rattly old car.)

"That is a cool sign," said Sam. "Have you been selling lots of lemonade?"

"Well, Nannie bought two cups. And Hannie and Linny each bought one," I replied. Hmm. Business was not booming.

"How about a couple of cups for your big brothers?" said Charlie.

He handed me two dimes. I knew they were buying my lemonade because they felt sorry for me. I made sure to fill their cups to the very top.

"If you like my lemonade, do not forget to tell your friends," I said.

A little while later a car pulled up to the curb. A man and a woman were sitting in front. Three kids were in back. The woman got out and asked for five cups of lemonade. She handed me fifty cents. Yes!!!

Two people walked by after that. They each bought a cup. Then I began waiting again. And waiting. It was hot. I was bored. Finally around four o'clock Kristy came outside with David Michael. They were wearing Krushers' uniforms and carrying lots of softball equipment.

"It is time for practice," said Kristy.

18

"Would you like to buy some lemonade before I put it away? It is really delicious," I said.

Kristy handed me two dimes. I had earned one dollar and fifty cents — in three whole hours. Boo and bullfrogs.

I ran into the house and put on my uniform. I was not sorry it was time to leave.

5

Kristy's Advice

"Batter up!" called Kristy.

We were on the grounds of Stoneybrook Elementary School. Kristy had divided the Krushers into two teams for practice. That made ten kids on each side.

Jamie Newton was first at bat. He is four years old.

The pitcher was David Michael. (He is one of the main pitchers for the Krushers. Nicky Pike, who is eight, is the other.) David Michael pulled back his arm, then threw the ball. It headed toward home plate.

Jamie jumped back. That is because he is afraid of the ball. On the second pitch, he ducked. On the third pitch, he practically ran away.

"Nice try," said Kristy. (Kristy is a very understanding coach.)

"You are up next, Karen," said Kristy.

I walked to home plate and picked up the bat.

"Go, Karen!" called Hannie and Nancy.

(Nancy does not like to play softball. But she comes to the games sometimes to help Kristy with the equipment.)

I stood waiting for the ball. I was tired of waiting. I had been waiting all day. I had been waiting for people to come buy my lemonade. Now I was waiting for the ball.

Whoosh! The ball passed right by me.

"Strike one!" called Kristy.

I had to stop thinking and start watching.

Whoosh! I missed the ball again.

When the third ball came, I was ready for it. I watched it come sailing toward me.

Whack! I hit it! I ran like the wind to first base.

But I tripped on the way. Luckily for me, the outfielders kept dropping the ball. I reached first base just in time.

"Way to go!" called Kristy.

Hannie was up next. I wanted her to hit the ball. If she did, I could run to second base.

Hannie swung and missed three times in a row. That strike out made three outs. I could not run to second base.

I put on my glove and took my place in the outfield. Not one ball came my way. There I was, waiting again. And thinking. I was thinking about my lemonade stand. I was wondering why hardly anyone had come.

I did not hit another ball for the rest of the practice. I dropped the two balls that finally came my way in the outfield because I was daydreaming. By the time practice was over I was in a gigundoly bad mood. I threw down my glove.

"Is something wrong?" asked Hannie.

"No, nothing is wrong. But you could have tried harder to hit the ball when I was on first base," I said.

I knew right away I should not have said that. Hannie had tried her best.

"That was mean," said Hannie. She stomped off.

Then Andrew ran to me. "Karen, would you tie my shoelace?" he asked.

"You know very well how to tie your shoelace. You are just being lazy," I snapped. Andrew looked hurt.

"Um, Karen. May I talk to you?" said Kristy. Kristy took me off to the side.

"What is *wrong*? You are snapping at everyone," she said.

"I am having a very bad day," I replied. "I am mad that hardly any customers came to my lemonade stand."

"That does not give you the right to be mean to Hannie and Andrew. You should

24

tell them you are sorry," said Kristy. "Now I will give you some advice about selling lemonade. If the customers do not come to you, then you must go to the customers."

Hmm. This sounded like a good idea. All I had to do was think about where the customers would be.

First I had some apologizing to do.

6

Ice Cold Lemonade

I was happy because Hannie and Andrew forgave me right away. I did not want them to be mad at me.

When I got home, I went to my room to have a talk with Moosie.

"Kristy says that if I want to sell lemonade, I have to go where the customers are," I explained. "Do you have any ideas?"

Moosie just sat there. I could tell he thought this was a very hard question. After all, who would want to be outside when it was a zillion degrees?

"Come on, Moosie. Help me think," I said.

Where had I seen a lot of people lately? People needed a reason to be outside when it was so hot. Where would they be going? What would they be doing?

Suddenly I had the answer. I had seen lots of people outside today. They were all at the school grounds. They were Kristy's Krushers!

"I can sell lemonade to the Krushers at softball practice, Moosie!" I said.

The kids on the team are not the only ones who come to practices. Parents and baby-sitters come with them. A lot of them stay to watch the game.

I would sell my lemonade to all those hot and thirsty people. I would sell it before and after each practice. I would sell it during the breaks, too.

Yippee! I ran to tell Kristy my plan.

"It sounds good," said Kristy. "Our next practice is on Thursday. Try it out and see how it goes."

On Thursday morning, I made a big batch of lemonade. (This time I let Nannie help me measure.) In the afternoon, Charlie drove Kristy, Andrew, and me to practice. Kristy was in charge of bringing the softball equipment. I was in charge of my lemonade stand. I had lemonade, the card table, plenty of napkins, cups, and my sign.

Charlie helped me set up the stand when we reached the schoolyard.

"Thank you, Charlie," I said. I gave him a free cup of lemonade for being so helpful.

We were the first ones at the school. But it was not long before kids started showing up with their parents and baby-sitters.

"Come and get it! Come and get your ice cold lemonade!" I called.

"Four cups, please," said a voice.

Was I hearing right? Did someone say *four* cups?

I looked up and saw Dawn Schafer. Dawn is in the Baby-sitters Club with Kristy. She had brought Buddy, Suzi, and Marnie Barrett to the practice. Buddy and

Suzi are on the team. Buddy is eight. Suzi is five. Marnie Barrett is two. She comes to watch almost all the games. She even has a Krushers' T-shirt.

"Four cups coming right up," I said.

Jamie Newton and his mother were next. Then Hannie, Linny, and David Michael came over. Nancy bought three cups, too. One was for her. The others were for her mother and her mother's friend.

Do you know what? People were lining up to buy my lemonade. It was hot outside. They were thirsty.

"Come and get it! Come and get your ice cold lemonade," I called.

I did it! I found the customers. I sold my lemonade at the break and after the game. I could hardly wait for the next practice to sell my lemonade again.

7

Be Back Soon

"Come on, Karen," said Kristy. "We are starting."

We were at the next practice. My lemonade stand was set up again. Business was booming. I wished I did not have to leave. I did not want to leave any thirsty customers behind.

I got an idea. I borrowed a pen from Nancy's mother. On the back of my sign I wrote in big letters BE BACK SOON. I hung up my new sign and returned the pen. Then

I grabbed my glove and took my place behind third base.

Matt Braddock was first at bat. Matt is an excellent softball player. He hit the ball on his first try. He ran all the way to third base.

The kids on his side cheered and signed, "Yea, Matt!" (Matt is deaf, so we use sign language to talk with him.)

I looked at the sidelines to see who was up next. It was Nina Marshall's turn. Nina is four. She is not a very good softball player. But she tries very hard.

While I was looking that way, I noticed Claire and Margo Pike eyeing the lemonade stand. They looked thirsty. I did not think they should have to wait for the break.

"I will be right back!" I called to my teammates.

I raced to the lemonade stand. Claire and Margo came running to me with their dimes.

I quickly turned over my sign so it said KAREN'S LEMONADE STAND again.

Then I poured two cups of lemonade. When I finished, I turned the sign over so it said BE BACK SOON. Then I returned to the outfield.

I watched two players at bat. They did not hit any balls. I peeked at my lemonade stand. Two grown-ups were standing there talking. They were probably getting thirsty talking in the heat.

I raced to the stand. On the way, I passed Kristy.

"I will be right back!" I called.

I turned over my sign so it said KAREN'S LEMONADE STAND again. The grown-ups each bought one cup.

"Your side is up at bat, Karen!" called Kristy.

I decided not to turn my sign over anymore. If anyone wanted lemonade I would run to the stand and serve them.

I grabbed a bat and raced to home plate.

"Here I am!" I said.

David Michael was pitching. The balls he was throwing were going wild. I did not swing at any of them. After four balls I got to walk to first base.

Oh, boy. While I was standing at first base, I saw someone at my lemonade stand. I thought about asking Hannie to take my place on first base. But I did not think Kristy would like that. Luckily for me the next three players struck out.

"I will be right back!" I called.

I raced to the stand and sold two more cups. By the end of the practice my money cup was filled with dimes.

The next practice was on Saturday. I spent even more time at the lemonade stand then. I was selling lemonade more than I was playing softball.

During the break, Kristy came to the stand to talk to me.

"What if a ball is hit to the outfield when you are not there? You will let down your teammates."

I could tell she was angry. And she was right about letting down my team. So I made an important decision.

"I am going to quit the team for a while," I announced. "My lemonade stand needs me full time."

"Are you sure?" asked Kristy.

"I am sure," I replied.

Playing softball was fun. But selling lemonade was even more fun than that.

Bobby's Stand

"Come and get it! Come and get your ice cold lemonade!" I called.

It was my first day as a full-time lemonade sales person. I had set up everything by the time kids started arriving with their parents and baby-sitters. I was lucky because it was hot and sunny again. That meant everyone was going to be thirsty.

"Hi, Karen," said Bobby Gianelli.

Bobby lives near the little house. He is in my class at school.

Bobby and his father were doing something interesting. They were setting up a table next to mine. Hmm.

"Are you going to sell lemonade, too?" I asked.

I was worried. Bobby used to be a bully. Now he is nice most of the time. But it would not be nice if he set up his own lemonade stand near mine.

"I am not going to sell lemonade," Bobby replied. "I am going to sell chocolate chip cookies."

"Cool!" I said. "Cookies and lemonade are very delicious together."

Bobby got everything ready. Then he called, "Cookies! Chocolate chip cookies here!"

"Lemonade! Ice cold lemonade here!" I called.

Wow! Kids did not walk over. They ran! They were hopping from one stand to the other. They were buying cookies *and* lemonade. It was a good thing I had made extra lemonade for my first full day on the job.

"Practice is starting, team," called Kristy.

"I have to go," said Bobby. "See you at the break."

I watched the game and took care of some customers. Bobby was back in no time. We sold cookies and lemonade during the break. Then Bobby closed his stand again. When the game was over, he reopened it. We kept our stands open until the last person left the field.

At the next practice, Bobby set up his stand next to mine again.

"We are ready to start the game, team," called Kristy.

"Um, Kristy, can I talk to you for a minute?" asked Bobby.

He talked to Kristy, then ran back to his stand.

"I quit the team," said Bobby. "I am now a full-time sales person, too."

When the game ended, Hannie came to keep me company.

"Can I help you?" she asked.

"Sure," I replied.

I was glad Hannie wanted to help me.

38

Business had been good that day. My arm was gigundoly tired from pouring lemonade. We took turns.

"This is fun," said Hannie. "Maybe I will open a stand, too. I could sell my homemade friendship bracelets."

"You could set up a table next to mine," I said. "That would be so great!"

"What would be so great?" asked Kristy from behind me.

"Hannie might open a stand," I replied.

"I am thinking about selling friendship bracelets," said Hannie.

"Oh," said Kristy. "Come on, Karen. It is time to go."

Kristy looked disappointed. First I quit the team. Then Bobby quit. If Hannie opened a stand, she would probably quit the team, too.

This was not good news for Kristy.

9

Melody's Pool

"*The temperature just hit the one hundred degree mark, Connecticut.*"

"Oh, no, not again," I said. "It is *so* hot out."

It was Saturday. I was having lunch with my big-house family. It had been three days since the last softball practice. No softball practice meant no lemonade stand. No lemonade stand meant I stayed inside. Inside it was air-conditioned.

These hot days were getting to be just

like rainy days. One is fun. Two are okay. Three or more are bor-ing!

"I am going to call Hannie," I announced. "Maybe she will be brave enough to go outside with me."

Hannie and I decided to call Melody Korman. We invited ourselves over to swim in her pool. Melody is seven. Her brother, Bill, is nine. They live across the street with their baby sister. Melody told me to bring my brothers, too.

I put on my pink bathing suit, a big purple T-shirt, and my blue pool shoes. I was feeling better already.

Hannie rang the bell. Linny was with her. The five of us went to Melody and Bill's house. Wow! I was glad we had called. Half the neighborhood was there.

"Hi, Mr. and Mrs. Korman," I said.

"Welcome to the party," Mr. Korman replied.

(Mr. and Mrs. Korman always stay outside to watch the kids who are in their pool.)

I took off my pool shoes and threw my T-shirt on a chair. Then I held my nose and jumped into the deep end.

"Who wants to play Marco Polo?" asked Melody.

All the kids did. Marco Polo is fun. Whoever is "it" closes his eyes and calls out "Marco!" The other kids have to answer "Polo!" That way the person who is it can hear where the other kids are and try to tag them. Whoever is tagged gets to be it.

Linny was it first.

"Marco!" he called.

"Polo!" we answered.

I was safe at the far end of the pool. Then Linny started heading in my direction.

"Marco!" he called.

"Polo!"

"Marco!"

"Polo!"

He got me! I was the next it.

We played Marco Polo for awhile. Then we played follow-the-leader in the water.

That was fun, too. We did silly strokes and underwater tricks.

While we were playing, the sky grew very dark. Then all of a sudden there was a flash of lightning.

"Everyone out of the pool and into the house, please," said Mrs. Korman.

By the time we had hurried inside, we heard thunder rumbling. Then more lightning flashed.

"Maybe we will finally get a storm that cools things off," said Mr. Korman.

We waited and wished for the storm to come. But it never did. This was the third time we had seen lightning and heard thunder, but no rain had come to cool us off.

When the sky grew bright, we went outside and played in the pool again. Then we went back home to our air-conditioned houses.

I wondered if the heat wave was ever going to end.

10

Kristy's Question

"Come and get your ice cold lemonade!" I called.

"Get your chocolate chip cookies!" called Bobby.

"Get your homemade friendship bracelets here!" called Hannie.

We were at a Krushers' practice. The game had not started yet.

"Hey, team. Would you come over here, please?" said Kristy. "I have something to tell you."

The kids gathered around. Bobby, Han-

45

nie, and I listened, too. Kristy was going to tell us something important.

"I have decided that we should play a World Series against Bart's Bashers," said Kristy.

(Bart Taylor is Kristy's age. I happen to think that she has a crush on him.)

"We will have to work hard if we want to beat the Bashers. That will make our practices a lot more fun," said Kristy.

Kristy led the Krushers in a team cheer.

"Are we ready to get to work?"

"Yes!"

"Are we going to work hard?"

"Yes!"

"Are we going to beat the Bashers?"

Only a couple of kids shouted "Yes!" The rest of the team looked kind of scared. We have played lots of games against the Bashers. We even played a World Series and won. But mostly the Bashers are better than us.

"I know the Bashers are a little older than you guys. But we can win if we try hard. Now I want to hear that team spirit," said Kristy. "Are we going to beat the Bashers?"

"Yes!" (I shouted "yes" too even though I was not a Krusher anymore.)

The practice was just starting when Nancy showed up. She was dragging a big shopping bag and a little folding table.

"Guess what. I have decided to be a salesperson," said Nancy. "I have to go help Kristy with the equipment now. I will see you at the break."

Nancy ran to the field and lined up the bats for the players. She made sure there were enough balls in the ball bucket. She handed out gloves to any player who needed one.

As soon as Kristy called for the break, Nancy grabbed the table. She opened it up next to Hannie's.

"What are you selling?" I asked.

Trail Mix

"You will see," replied Nancy.

She dragged the shopping bag to the table. Then she started pulling out armloads of small plastic bags. Each bag was filled with trail mix and tied with a colored ribbon. Nancy lined the bags up on her table and called, "Trail mix! Trail mix for sale."

"Ooh. Cool idea," I said.

We did great business over the break. Then Nancy helped out Kristy during the second half of the practice. When it was over, she returned to her trail mix stand.

"Trail mix. Get your trail mix here!" she called.

Soon Kristy appeared. "I thought you were going to help me put the equipment away," she said.

"Um, I would like to talk to you," said Nancy.

"I know," said Kristy. "You quit."

"That is right," said Nancy. "I am sorry."

"So am I," replied Kristy. "If everyone quits the team, how are we going to play a World Series game?"

This was a very good question. No one had a very good answer.

11

Clunk! Thunk. Zap.

Clunk! Thunk. Zap.

"Oh, no!" I cried.

"This is terrible," said Elizabeth.

"I will call the repair service," said Daddy.

The air-conditioning in the big house had broken down. It was already ninety-six degrees outside. I listened to Daddy talking on the phone.

"We need someone to come over here right away," said Daddy. He listened for a minute. Then he said, "Oh, I see."

"What happened? Are they coming right over?" I asked.

"I am afraid not," replied Daddy. "The company is overloaded with phone calls today. Everyone needs repairs. They would not even put us on their waiting list."

"I will get the phone book," said Elizabeth. "There must be a company who can help us out."

Daddy and Elizabeth took turns calling every repair service in the book. A few of them took our name and said they would call back. But Daddy said we should not count on getting the air-conditioning fixed very soon.

"All right," said Elizabeth. "Here is Plan B. We go into town to buy air conditioners or fans that we can install in the windows. Who wants to come along?"

"I do!" I said.

So did everyone else. If we went shopping, we could go from the air-conditioned car to the air-conditioned stores.

We put down big bowls of fresh cold water for Shannon and Boo-Boo. (We figured our other pets would be okay until we came home.) Then we piled into the mini van.

We started at Bellair's Department Store.

"Sorry. We are all sold out of air conditioners and fans," said the salesperson.

We got the same news at every store in town.

"It is time for Plan C," said Elizabeth.

"What is that?" asked Daddy.

"I do not know yet," Elizabeth replied. "We will think of something on the way home."

By the time we returned to the house, we had Plan C. It was not great. But it was the best we could do. The plan was this: Anything goes!

We all ran around the house opening windows and putting up screens.

Sam and Charlie helped Daddy drag a few old, rinky-dink fans down from the attic.

We took turns taking cold showers. (Kristy was the timer. Three minutes per person.)

We drank a lot of lemonade. (I was the lemonade mixer, of course.)

I made paper fans from old newpapers. (I was too hot to decorate them.)

The Kormans let us use their pool a lot. Our friends let us visit a lot.

You know what? We had fun. (Sort of.) But at night, we had a big problem. Really we had a lot of little problems. Bugs. Nannie called them no-see-ems. They were attracted to the lights and they were tiny enough to get through our screens.

They were everywhere!

"Here is our choice," said Nannie. "If we open the windows so we stay cool, we will have to keep the lights off so the bugs stay away. If we leave the lights on so we can see, we will have to close the windows to keep the bugs out."

I was not having fun anymore. And it was two more days before the air-conditioning was repaired.

12

Making Plans

It was a Thursday morning. Kristy had called for an early practice. That is because it is usually cooler before noon.

Nannie drove us to the school grounds in the Pink Clinker. (That is the name of her car.)

I set up my stand in the same spot as always. There were now six of us who had quit the team and were full-time salespeople. Here was the line-up: Bobby selling chocolate chip cookies; me selling ice cold lemonade; Hannie selling homemade friendship bracelets; Nancy selling tasty trail mix; Nicky selling fresh popcorn; Margo selling paper fans.

"Practice is starting, team!" called Kristy.

There were only fourteen kids left on the team. More than half of them were at our stands asking us questions. They wanted to find out about opening up stands of their own.

We told them about tables and signs and having plenty to sell.

"Business is very good," I said.

Jackie Rodowsky's dad was buying some lemonade and popcorn. (Jackie is on the Krushers' team. He is seven.)

"These stands are really terrific," said Mr. Rodowsky. "Have you kids thought about pooling your talents?"

"What does that mean?" I asked.

"It means that you could *all* set up stands together somewhere," Mr. Rodowsky replied. "You could hold a food and crafts fair."

"What a neat idea!" I said.

Everyone liked it. Everyone except Kristy.

"What about practice?" she asked. "What about the World Series?"

I felt bad. No one was listening to Kristy. The kids were all talking about holding a fair. We were excited about making our plans.

"We should make a list of other things to sell," suggested David Michael.

"I bet we could hold the fair right here," said Hannie.

"When should we do it?" asked Nancy.

We wrote down what each person wanted to sell. Mr. Rodowsky promised to find out if we could hold the fair on the school grounds. We decided the fair would be held a week from Saturday.

"What will we do if it rains?" asked Andrew.

"Rain? What is that?" I said.

Everyone thought this was funny. It had been so long since it had rained we could hardly remember what rain was.

We set a rain date for two weeks from Saturday just in case.

Kristy was sitting alone up in the bleachers. I felt bad for her. But I really wanted to hold the fair. It was going to be so much fun!

13

Helping Hannie

"*The heat wave continues. The temperature is expected to reach one hundred degrees again today. It is hot and dry. We need to save water. Keep your showers short. Do not water plants or lawns. This is Margie Simon reporting.*"

I turned off the TV. I decided I might not want to be a weather reporter after all. There was an awful lot of bad weather news. And it was the same old thing day after day.

"See you later, everyone," I said to my family.

It was early Friday morning. The fair was going to be held the next day. I had promised Hannie I would come over as early as I could to help her make friendship bracelets.

"I will see you over there in a little while," said Kristy. "Mr. and Mrs. Papadakis are going to New York City for the day. I will be baby-sitting until they get back in the evening."

There was no Krushers' practice. And the World Series was on hold. That is because kids were busy getting ready for the fair.

Hannie was very excited about the fair. She was ready to work, and had laid everything out on the floor in her room.

"Welcome to the Friendship Factory," she said. "Home of Hannie's world-famous friendship bracelets."

"We better get started," I said. "I have to report back to my world-famous lemonade factory this afternoon."

In a little while, we heard Kristy arrive. Then Hannie's parents poked their heads in the room to say good-bye.

"Have fun and keep cool, girls," said Mrs. Papadakis.

"We are cool," I replied. "Way cool!"

Hannie gave her parents hugs. After they left, she said, "Do you think Kristy would like to help us make bracelets? I could use as much help as I can get."

"You could ask her if you like," I said. "But Kristy is not in such a good mood lately. She is pretty upset that her team quit. And she is unhappy with me because I started the whole thing with my lemonade stand."

"We can make the bracelets by ourselves," said Hannie quickly.

We worked hard all morning. And we had fun. The bracelets looked gigundoly beautiful. My favorite was the green, pink, and white one that I made.

"I think I will buy this tomorrow at the fair," I said.

"Really? I will buy lots of lemonade from you," said Hannie.

We worked until Kristy called us for

lunch. She had made peanut butter and jelly sandwiches for us. But she did not keep us company while we ate them.

By midafternoon Hannie had filled a box with beautiful bracelets.

"I am going home now," I said. "I have to make several batches of lemonade for tomorrow."

"Thank you for helping me," said Hannie. "I will see you in the morning. I can hardly wait!"

"Me, too," I replied.

I waved to Kristy on my way out. She was in the living room playing with Sari. She waved back, but she did not smile at me.

When I walked outside it did not look like afternoon at all. It looked like nighttime. That is because the sky was very dark. Hannie and I had been so busy making bracelets we did not notice what was happening.

Instead of making lemonade when I got home, I ran straight to the TV room. My big-house family was there listening to Margie Simon's weather report.

"We have severe storm warnings in effect for Connecticut. Stay tuned for updates throughout the afternoon," she said.

Hmm. Things were getting exciting. Maybe I would be a weather reporter after all.

Storm Warnings

I never made my lemonade. By four o'clock, storm warnings were being broadcast on every radio and TV station. The weather reporters were talking about monstrous thunderstorms, hail, dangerous lightning, even possible tornados.

"The storm warning now extends through midnight. Stay tuned," said Margie Simon.

"It sounds as though a storm is really coming this time," said Daddy. "We need to get ready for it."

"I will call Kristy at the Papadakises' and tell her to do the same thing," said Elizabeth.

We brought in everything from outside that could possibly blow away. Nannie went around unplugging appliances so we would not have lightning fires.

"I will go to the store," said Charlie. "We need things in case the power goes out. I will get extra batteries, flashlights, bottled water, and canned food. Does anyone want to come along?"

"I do!" I said.

"Me, too," said David Michael.

Elizabeth called Kristy again to see if she needed anything from the store. Kristy said she did not think so. She said Mr. and Mrs. Papadakis were due home in just a few hours.

Going to town was exciting. The stores were filled with people rushing around buying things for the storm, just like my brothers and I were doing. I even ran into a few people I knew.

"Hi, Mr. Korman! Are you buying batteries? Are Melody and Bill here?" I asked.

"Hello, Karen. Yes, I am buying batteries. But Melody and Bill did not come with me," Mr. Korman replied.

"Say hi to them for me," I said.

David Michael and I were lucky. We got to go on this exciting and important assignment.

We bought batteries and flashlights at the hardware store. (I picked out pretty flashlights. They were yellow, bright green, and hot pink. I found them in a basket for a dollar apiece.)

Then we went to the supermarket.

"Can we get popcorn?" I asked. "I think we are all out of it."

"We are not shopping for a party, Karen," said Charlie. "We are shopping for a storm. That means we need real food, not just snacks."

"We can watch the storm out the window while we are eating popcorn. It will be dark just like at the movies," I said.

"Oh, all right. Grab some popcorn since we need it anyway," said Charlie.

The line at the checkout counter was long. But I did not mind. I talked to lots of people.

By the time we returned to the big house, the sky was dark and green. It looked like pea soup. Thunder was rumbling. The air was still. Ooh, spooky!

The Storm

*F*lash! That was lightning.

Boom! That was thunder.

The storm started with a few drops of rain around six-thirty. Then it got bigger and bigger.

Woof! Woof!

"Shannon, off!" called David Michael.

David Michael was sitting on the couch in the TV room when Shannon jumped onto his lap.

Shannon is only a puppy. But she is a very big puppy. She weighs about

70

ninety pounds. Shannon is scared of storms.

So is Andrew. He did not jump into my lap. But he followed me all over the house and tugged on my sleeve a lot.

I did not mind, though. I am very brave in storms. I think they are gigundoly exciting.

Flash! Boom!

Emily started to cry. Nannie picked her up and rocked her.

I heard a groaning sound that seemed to come from inside the walls. Then the lights went out.

You know what? I was glad Andrew was hanging on to me then. I am brave in storms. But I am not so brave when the lights go out. And the air-conditioning goes off.

"Where are those flashlights, Charlie?" called Daddy.

"I thought I put them down here in the kitchen," replied Charlie. "But I cannot find them."

Oh, boy. We needed flashlights to find our flashlights.

"I wish we could call Kristy to make sure everything is all right over there," said Elizabeth. "But the phones are out, too."

"I will go across the street," said Daddy. "I do not think Kristy and the kids should be alone over there."

Daddy opened the door. Then he closed it again.

"The lightning looks too dangerous now. I will just have to wait until the storm settles down a bit," said Daddy.

Flash! Boom! We wondered how long that would be.

16

A Party

Finally the storm quieted down. Andrew let go of my sleeve. Emily stopped crying. Shannon came out from under the table. (That is where she went when David Michael put her down.)

It was still rainy and dark. But there was much less thunder and lightning. Charlie had found the flashlights, so I was not scared anymore.

"I will try going across the street again," said Daddy.

He put on a rain slicker. But as soon as he opened the door Kristy, Hannie, Linny, and Sari rushed inside. Their pets Pat the Cat, Myrtle the Turtle, and Noodle the Poodle were with them. (Their pets and our pets get along fine except for cranky Boo-Boo. He just keeps to himself.)

"Wow!" said Kristy. "This storm is amazing. I decided to hurry over as soon as it calmed down."

"Hi, Hannie!" I said. "Were you scared?"

"I was a little scared when I found out the phone did not work," Hannie replied.

"Kristy, did you hear from Mr. and Mrs. Papadakis before the phone went out?" asked Elizabeth.

"No," Kristy replied. "I guess they will not be able to return until tomorrow. We packed some things so we can stay here tonight."

"That was a very good idea," said Daddy.

(I told you Kristy is an excellent baby-sitter.)

For dinner we ate leftovers from the refrigerator. Even though the power was out, everything was still pretty cold.

"I hope my parents are okay in the storm," said Hannie. She looked worried.

"I am sure they are fine," replied Elizabeth. "They are probably in a hotel. That is a safe place to be."

After dinner, we played a game of flashlight charades. Everyone shined their flashlights on the person giving the clues. It was fun. When it was my turn, I felt as if I were a movie star.

Later, Kristy told a ghost story about a teeny tiny woman who lived in a teeny tiny house and found a teeny tiny bone that she put into her teeny tiny cupboard. It was not a scary ghost story. It was funny.

Then Hannie and I went to my room. Elizabeth helped us set up a cot. Then she left us to play.

"Let's pretend we are pioneer girls," I said. "We are out on the prairie at night. It is dark because we have no electricity.

We do not have phones because they have not been invented yet."

"I would have to get on my horse and ride over to your house to talk," said Hannie. "Giddy-up!"

She trotted around my room. Suddenly there was another flash of lightning followed by booming thunder. Hannie dived onto the cot and covered her head with pillows.

"I guess I am not such a brave pioneer girl after all," she said.

We started giggling. We were so loud that Daddy came to check on us. When he saw we were all right he said, "I guess I cannot tell you to turn out the lights tonight. They are not on. But it is late and time to go to sleep."

"Can we read for a little while?" I asked.

"Of course," Daddy replied. "And if you get scared in the night, just call and I will come keep you company."

I went to my bookcase and pulled out my copy of *Little House on the Prairie*. Hannie

and I took turns reading out loud. We read by flashlight.

The rain was still beating on the windows of my room. But the storm did not feel scary anymore. It was a cozy storm now.

17

What a Mess

When I woke up on Saturday morning the storm was over and the sun was shining. Hannie was still asleep. I got up quietly and looked out the window. I could see that we would not be having the fair. Our yard and the streets were a complete mess.

Whole trees were lying across the road. There were fallen branches everywhere. Clean-up and repair crews were already at work.

I tried turning on a light to see if the power had returned. It had not.

Yawn. Stretch. Hannie was waking up.

"Good morning," she said. "Is the storm over?"

"It is over. But Stoneybrook is a mess. Come look," I replied.

Hannie came to the window.

"Wow. It really is a mess," she said.

We got dressed and went downstairs to eat breakfast. A battery-operated radio was turned on in the kitchen.

"Yesterday's storm left heavy damage in our area. For your safety, be sure to stay away from all power lines that are down. Repair crews will be working round the clock to fix them," said the announcer.

"The phone is still out," said Kristy. "I picked it up and there was no dial tone."

"I am sure everything will be fixed soon," said Elizabeth. "Here are your choices for breakfast. You can have dry cereal with apple juice to wash it down. There is peanut butter, jelly, bread, and fruit. You may also have anything in cans that will not give you a bellyache this early in the morning."

Nannie and Charlie had already eaten. They were busy cleaning out the refrigerator and freezer. Almost everything had to be thrown out.

I decided to have Krispy Krunchy cereal and a cup of apple juice. It was a fine breakfast.

After we ate we ran across the street to check on the Papadakises' house.

"Uh-oh," said Hannie. "More mess."

The window shutters from Hannie's room were scattered in pieces on the ground. Two downstairs windows were broken. A stray garbage can was overturned on the grass. And the welcome mat that said *Papadakis* on it had disappeared completely.

"We better get busy," said Daddy. "We have two yards to clean up."

"It is a good thing we made a rain date for the fair," said David Michael.

"It is not a rain date anymore," I said. "It is a *storm* date."

It would have been fun to have had the

fair. But I was not too disappointed. Hannie and I were going to pretend that we were brave and helpful pioneer girls again.

Our first job was to clean up the prairie.

Good News

In a few hours both yards looked almost as good as new.

"Now what are we going to do?" I asked.

"Sam and I are going for a walk," replied Kristy. "We want to see what happened in the other neighborhoods."

"Can Hannie and I come along?" I said.

"Sure," replied Sam.

David Michael and Linny wanted to come, too. We asked Daddy and Elizabeth if it would be okay.

"Yes, you may go," said Daddy. "Just

remember the warning we heard on the radio. Power lines are very dangerous and you must stay away from them."

"Walk only on main streets and dry land," said Elizabeth. "Any water you find may be deeper than you think."

"Be sure you all stick together," said Nannie.

They had a long list of warnings. We promised to be careful on our walk.

The other neighborhoods looked a lot like ours. Some blocks were a little better. Some were a little worse.

"That car looks like a pancake!" I said. I pointed to a squashed car across the street.

"A tree must have fallen on it and been removed," said Sam.

We pointed out all the strange things we saw. We found three garages with no roof-tops and two more pancake cars.

We walked until we reached the Stoney-brook Elementary School playground.

"Oh no!" cried David Michael. "Check out the bleachers. They are ruined!"

The bleachers had been smashed by a huge tree. The tree was lying where it had fallen.

"That does it. No more games. No World Series," said Kristy. "I guess no one would have come to the World Series anyway."

Kristy looked gigundoly sad. She stood staring at the mess that used to be our bleachers.

Hannie and I sat on the swings. (They had not been damaged by the storm.)

"I feel bad for Kristy," I said. "She had her heart set on having a World Series."

"Maybe the school will rebuild the bleachers," said Hannie.

"They probably do not have enough money," I said. "I am sure it costs a lot."

"I have an idea," said Hannie. "We could help raise the money to build new bleachers. We could donate the money we make at our fair."

"What a cool idea!" I replied. "After that, we could join the Krushers again. Kristy could have her World Series after all."

86

"You know, I miss playing softball," said Hannie. "I am kind of sick of making friendship bracelets."

Hannie and I did not tell Kristy our idea right away. We wanted to talk to the other Krushers first.

Luckily, the phones were working by the time we got home. And Hannie's parents had returned. We each made phone calls from our houses.

At the end of the day, I went to Kristy's room.

"I have good news," I said.

I told her our plan to raise money to build the new bleachers.

"And all the Krushers want to join the team again," I said. "That way we can play in the World Series."

Kristy smiled at me.

"Thanks, little sister," she said.

"You are welcome, big sister," I replied.

19

The Fair

The next Saturday the sun was shining and we held our fair.

"Come and get it! Come and get your ice cold lemonade," Andrew called. (Andrew is too little to have his own booth. So I let him help with mine.)

The heat wave had ended with the storm. But we were still selling plenty of lemonade.

When word got out that the fair was for a good cause, more kids in the neighborhood signed up. There were stands everywhere you looked.

"I will see you later," said Andrew. "I want to walk around the fair with Kristy."

I was having a very good time being a salesperson. But I wanted to walk around the fair, too.

"Come on," I said to Hannie and Nancy. "Let's go see what the other kids are selling."

The Three Musketeers put up "Be Back Soon" signs. We brought the money we had earned so far to Kristy. She was one of the bankers for the fair. Then we walked around the school grounds.

These are the things I bought: A yo-yo from Matt's toy stand; a key ring on a braided lanyard from Melody and Bill; and two paperback books from Jamie. (David Michael was selling baseball cards, but I did not want any of those.)

"Three throws for a dime!" called Buddy. "Step right up."

Buddy and Suzi had made a game stand. I tried to throw a Ping-Pong ball into a clown's mouth. There were no prizes, but if I won I could play another game for free.

I love games like that. I am very good at them, too. You know what? I won!

"Do you want to take my free game?" I asked Hannie. (Nancy was looking for her parents and her brother.)

"Sure. Thanks, Karen," Hannie replied.

When we finished walking around the fair, I still had a little money left over. I dropped it into the donation box where money was being collected to help rebuild the bleachers. Then I returned to my lemonade stand.

Matt's mother was helping with the fair. At three o'clock she made an announcement.

"Our fair is coming to a close. Please bring us any money you would like to donate," she said.

I dropped the rest of the money I had

earned into the donation box. Then I went back to my stand.

"Come and get your *free* ice cold lemonade!" I called. I had not started my business to make money. I just wanted to have fun. I served my lemonade until it was all gone.

At four o'clock everyone gathered in front of what was left of the bleachers.

"Thank you for working so hard to raise money to rebuild the Stoneybrook Elementary School bleachers," said Mrs. Braddock.

She told us that we had made several hundred dollars. This was not enough to rebuild the bleachers right away, but everyone agreed it was a very good start.

It was time to pack up our stands. My selling days were over for a while. I did not mind. My friends did not mind either. We were ready to play softball again.

20

The World Series

"*Our team is red hot! Your team is all shot!*"

It was the Saturday of the World Series. The Krushers were ready to go to bat. There were no bleachers of course. But there was still a big crowd at the Stoneybrook Elementary School grounds.

My big-house family had come to watch. They had brought lawn chairs and blankets to sit on. A lot of other people had done the same thing.

"I cannot believe how many people

showed up," said Kristy. She looked very happy.

She looked even happier when Bart Taylor, the Bashers' coach, came to talk to her. (She always looks happy when she is talking to Bart.) I heard them discussing the game rules.

The Krushers are a special kind of team, so we have special kinds of rules. For example, we play seven innings instead of nine. The littlest kids get to play with a Whiffle ball instead of the softball. And everyone has to remember to sign to Matt.

"You are up first, Karen," said Kristy.

Yes! I turned to my family and waved. Being the first batter was an important job. If I did well, I would put the Krushers in a good mood. If they were in a good mood, they would probably win. It would all be thanks to me.

"Go, Karen!" called Hannie and Nancy when I walked up to the plate.

I felt a little nervous. I felt like there were butterflies in my stomach. I was glad when

Kristy put her arm around me and whispered, "Just stay calm and do your best."

A kid named Jerry was pitching for the Bashers. He kept doing funny things such as winding up his arm and making believe he was spitting on his hand. (I hoped he was just kidding.)

"Come on, Jerry. Play ball!" called Kristy.

The next thing I knew the ball was flying my way. I swung at it and missed. Boo.

"Strike one!" called Bart.

"That is okay," said Kristy. "Just keep your eye on the ball and you will do fine."

I kept my eye on the next ball. It did not look like a very good pitch, so I let it go by.

"Ball one!" called Bart.

"Good eye, Karen," said Kristy.

The next ball came sailing toward home plate. I swung my bat. I hit the ball!

I ran to first base. I ran to second base. I reached second base just before the ball did.

"Safe!" called Bart.

My family and all the Krushers were jumping up and down and cheering for me.

Matt was up next. He hit the very first ball way out in the field. I ran to third base then headed for home. I scored the first run of the game.

"Way to go!" called Hannie and Nancy.

The Krushers were in a great mood. We hit one ball after another. We won the game by two runs. The score was six to four.

When the game was over the Krushers made a circle around Kristy, our coach.

Our team is red hot! The best coach is what we've got!

The heat wave was over. The Krushers had won the World Series. And we knew that soon we would have brand new bleachers.

Yea, team!

About the Author

ANN M. MARTIN lives in New York City and loves animals, especially cats. She has two cats of her own, Mouse and Rosie.

Other books by Ann M. Martin that you might enjoy are *Stage Fright*; *Me and Katie (the Pest)*; and the books in *The Baby-sitters Club* series.

Ann likes ice cream and *I Love Lucy*. And she has her own little sister, whose name is Jane.

Little Sister

Don't miss #65

KAREN'S TOYS

Andrew gave me a funny look. I squeezed his hand to make sure he did not say anything.

We walked across the toy store to the *Space Game* display. Daddy stayed at the counter talking with Mr. Mellon.

"I do not understand," said Andrew. "How can you buy these toys for us? We are not allowed to have them."

"It will be okay as long as we leave them at the big house," I replied. "You just have to promise not to tell Mommy or Seth about them. The toys will be our secret."

Andrew did not look too happy about keeping a secret from Mommy and Seth. Then his eyes fell on the ray-sprayer. I knew he wanted it.

"Okay," he said. "I promise not to tell."

If you like the **Baby-sitters Little Sister** books
you'll love

THE KIDS IN MS. COLMAN'S CLASS

A new series by Ann M. Martin

Don't miss #1
TEACHER'S PET

Nancy looked down the hallway. She knew where her room was. She walked toward it very slowly. Natalie ran by her. Omar ran by her. Ricky ran by her.

"Hey, slowpoke!" Ricky called to Nancy.

Nancy stopped outside Ms. Colman's room. She poked her head in the door.

"BOO!" shouted Bully Bobby.

"Aughh!" shrieked Nancy.

"Scared you, you baby," said Bobby. He glared at Nancy.

Nancy took another step into the room. She saw Natalie, Ricky, the Barkan twins, and some other kids she knew from kindergarten and first grade. And she saw a lot of kids she did not know.

"Good morning, boys and girls," said a grown-up's voice.

Standing in the doorway behind Nancy was Ms. Colman. She was smiling. She was smiling even though Ian Johnson was pretending to brush his hair with an eraser. And even though Audrey Green was giving herself a tattoo with a red Magic Maker. And even though Hank Reubens was tickling Leslie Morris and had made Leslie fall on the floor.

Nancy looked at Hannie. She was about to lean over and whisper, "Psst! Hey! Hannie Papadakis!"

But Hannie was busy whispering to Sara Ford who sat in front of her. Then Terri Barkan turned around and asked Hannie if she could borrow a pencil. And then Ricky passed a note to Hannie.

Nancy sighed. She gazed around the room. Who would be her second-grade best friend?

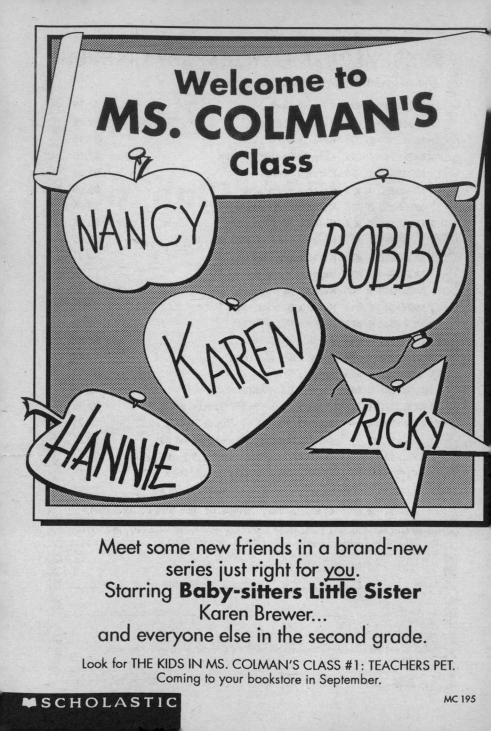